I WILL BE THERE

Written by
DIANA ALEKSANDROVA

Illustrated by
VICTORIA MARBLE

Hardcover ISBN: 978-1-953118-23-3
Paperback ISBN: 978-1-953118-22-6

Library of Congress Control Number: 2022904798

Published by Dedoni, LLC
www.dedonibooks.com

IN LOVING MEMORY OF
RAYMOND P ODREY

The day I heard your first soft cries,
a flood of tears filled my eyes.
I made a **promise** that each day:
I will be there to lead your way.

I'll be there when you learn to crawl,
to hold your hand and break your fall.
You may get scared; you may be sad.
I'll 'have your back' - good days or bad.

Each night I'll come to tuck you in,
then you can wake up with a grin.
I'll be there with my love for you,
so you will know, and share love, too.

I'll bring the candles for each cake,
and be there for each step you take.
I know you'll grow up good and strong.
You'll say you're sorry when you're wrong.

You know I'll always cheer for you,
for big achievements - small ones, too.
I'll show you awesome things to try.
I PROMISE YOU CAN REACH THE SKY!

I'll be there when you start new phase,
and give you strength with thoughtful praise.
To friends you'll be - both tried and true,
the way you want them treating you.

I'll be there with you by the fire.
and teach you nature to admire.
I'll keep you safe from awful things,
but give you space to 'spread your wings.'

I'll be there, so you'll know what's right-
when faced with darkness, find the light.
I'll teach you not to ever judge,
be fair, and never hold a grudge.

I'll come and relish your success,
but if you fail, I'm proud no less.
At times, you'll have to try again.
I know you'll be successful, then.

I'll be there when you leave the nest -
and help you choosing east or west.
I'll guide you, but the choice is yours:
Appreciate life's open doors.

Though far away, I'll be with you
at every milestone, that is true.
You work so hard, but don't forget,
a time for resting you should set.

And when I'm there for your big day,
I will support you all the way.

Your wealth is not a house and roof.
A happy family is the proof.

I'll be there when you 'take the leap' -
your vow of fatherhood to keep.
I'm really glad I taught you well.
In life, what matters, you can tell.

I'll be there. You are not alone -
no matter small, or fully grown.
I'm honored and so very glad,
to be there for you as your **DAD**!

Diana Aleksandrova is award-winning author of children books.

Diana's mission is to help emerging and reluctant readers fall in love with books. She believes that reading is the way to shape thinking and emotionally intelligent future generation.

From amazing empowering monster adventures to sweet rhyming stories - Too Cute to Spook and Mother's Love are some of her most known Picture Books.

Diana's illustrated **chapter books** are perfect for kids transitioning from Picture Books to longer text. Her fantasy adventures are created to keep the young reader's attention with illustrations throughout and a healthy blend of shivers and giggles.

You can reach Diana at dedonibooks.com

Victoria Marble is an illustrator specializing in character & narrative design, with a particular emphasis on children, animals, insects, & floral designs.

Victoria's love for drawing led her to pursue a well-rounded artistic background with courses completed in a wide range of concepts and media, including drawing and composition, figure drawing, painting, illustration, multimedia, and game design. Her artwork has won various awards.

Victoria's first illustrated works, Baum's Wonderful Wizard of Oz and Tux in the Zoo by Diana Aleksandrova, were published by MacLaren-Cochrane in 2019 and 2020 respectively.

Victoria adores creating art that emphasizes the beauty of nature- and particularly birds, fish, insects, and floral designs, along with cute children and animal characters. It is to the memory of her late father, Raymond Odrey, that I Will Be There is lovingly dedicated.

To see more of Victoria's artwork, visit victoriamarbleart.com

Made in the USA
Middletown, DE
11 June 2023

32419825R00018